A Secret Party
in Boston Harbor

Kris Hemphill

Illustrated by
John Martin
Cover Illustration by
Daniel Van Pelt

90837

SILVER MOON PRESS
NEW YORK

First Silver Moon Press Edition 1998
Copyright © 1998 by Kris Hemphill
Illustration Copyright © 1998 by John Martin and
Daniel Van Pelt
Edited by Theresa Desmond
Historical Fact Check by Carolyn Hughes

For information:
Silver Moon Press
New York, NY
(800) 874-3320

Library of Congress Cataloging-in-Publication Data
Hemphill, Kris, 1963-
A Secret Party in Boston Harbor/Kris Hemphill;
illustrated by Daniel Van Pelt.
p. cm. — (Mysteries in time)
Summary: Eleven-year-old Sarah Turner recalls the difficult
times for her family caused by the British presence in Boston in
the 1770s and the events leading up to the act of rebellion known
as the Boston Tea Party.
ISBN 1-881889-88-2: $13.95
1. Boston Tea Party, 1773 – Juvenile fiction. [1. Boston Tea
Party, 1773–Fiction. 2. Boston (Mass.)–History–Colonial period,
ca. 1600-1775–Fiction.] I. Van Pelt, Daniel, ill. II. Title. III. Series
PZ7.H37745Se   1998
[Fic] – dc21
98 - 10995
CIP
AC

10 9 8 7 6 5 4 3 2 1

Printed in the USA

To my husband, Scott–
you're the best.
And to Kevin, Brian, and Rachel,
with love.

TABLE OF CONTENTS

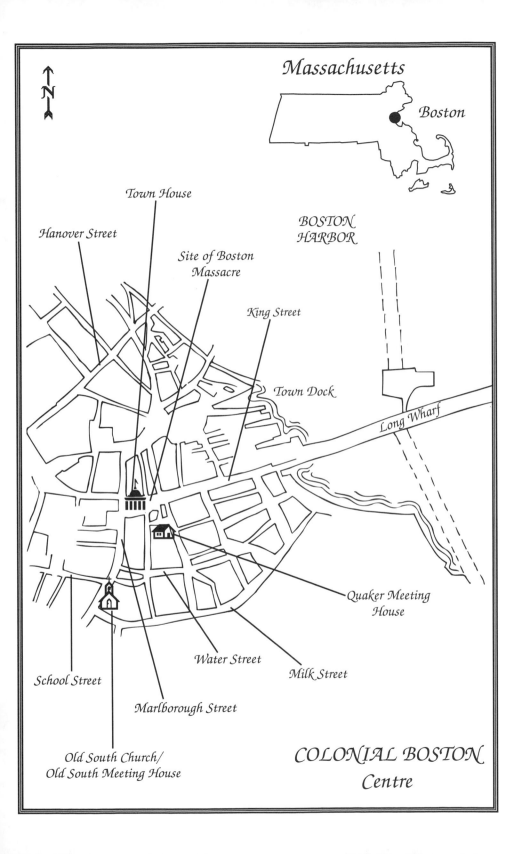

Massachusetts

Boston

Town House

Hanover Street

Site of Boston
Massacre

BOSTON
HARBOR

King Street

Town Dock

Long Wharf

Quaker Meeting
House

Water Street

Milk Street

School Street

Marlborough Street

Old South Church/
Old South Meeting House

COLONIAL BOSTON
Centre

1

THE MYSTERIOUS RED SCARF

A THIN STRAND OF AUBURN HAIR DANGLED down in front of Sarah Turner's nose as she scraped away at the grease inside the cast-iron kettles with a handful of sand. She blew the hair away as her arm continued its scrubbing motion. The vigorous work helped to keep her warm on this chilly October morning in 1773.

Sarah set down the kettle and grimaced at the sight of three more pots still waiting to be scoured.

"You'd best tend to the fire, Sarah, before the ashes grow cold," warned her mother.

"Yes, ma'am." Sarah wiped her hands on her apron, now blackened from grease, as she walked to the back door of the Maple Leaf Coffee House. Her parents, Seth and Isabel Turner, owned and operated the coffee house. It was located on King Street, the busiest street in Boston, Massachusetts.

"And mind you don't traipse mud inside," called

her mother. "The ground is a mite soft from last night's rain."

Sarah leaped over a puddle and landed on a patch of grass still damp from the morning dew. The cold air cut through her thin sleeves. Her ankle-length dress and petticoats offered little warmth for her long legs.

At the age of eleven, Sarah stood taller than most of the girls her age. Even when she attended Miss Cartwright's dame school at the age of seven, she could see over the head of John Williams, the tallest boy in the class. But no one dared tease her in school, for Sarah could read better and faster than any other pupil.

"You must learn to read and speak properly," her mother would say, "so you can carry on a lively conversation with our customers." And so, every night before bedtime, Sarah would join her parents in front of the fireplace in the kitchen. While her mother scraped kernels of corn from the cob and her father polished the brass buckles on his shoes, Sarah would read aloud her favorite passages from the family Bible. By the time she was nine, she could read the town newspaper, the *Boston Gazette,* from front to back.

Shivering from the cold, Sarah wrapped her arms tightly around her middle and headed toward the tall oak tree where the firewood was stored.

As she made her way toward the giant oak, Sarah noticed something red sitting atop the woodpile. She quickened her pace, anxious to see what it was. Wet leaves clung to the soles of her flimsy shoes as she approached the mysterious object.

Suddenly, she stopped. For there, on top of the heap of stacked logs, neatly folded, was a red scarf with a red ribbon tied around it.

Sarah gasped. She recognized it instantly as the scarf she had lost that terrifying night three years ago. Her body grew weak as she recalled the events of that fateful night—a night that had changed her life forever. . . .

It was March 5, 1770, a bitterly cold night. The wind howled and moaned, blowing snow from the coffee house's steeply angled roof. The rusty weathercock mounted on the roof twisted and turned with shrill creaks, sending a shiver down Sarah's spine. She snuffed out the last candle in the coffee house and walked to the door leading to the family kitchen.

Attached to the Maple Leaf Coffee House was the Turners' living space. It was small but large enough for Sarah and her parents. A single door located near the back of the shop's narrow dining room led to the Turners' kitchen. A great brick fireplace was the focal point in the room. Copper cooking utensils

3

decorated the wall, often reflecting the glowing light from the fireplace. Sarah's father kept his musket hanging above the mantle.

Sarah grabbed the brass warming pan from the hearth and filled it with hot coals. Wrapping her apron around the long handle, she heaved the weighty pan up the steep stairs of the wooden house.

Two modest bedchambers were situated above the kitchen. Sarah's chamber faced the front of the house. It was plain, but Sarah treasured the small, narrow window overlooking King Street. Every day she would look out and see the crooked, stone-paved street filled with men pushing carts, wagons, drays, and wheelbarrows. Occasionally, a carriage would thunder down the crowded street, nearly trampling an innocent traveler on foot. Now the streets were quiet as she moved the warming pan back and forth swiftly over her bed so as not to burn a hole in the linen sheets.

The warm bed felt heavenly as she snuggled down, pulling the layers of wool blankets and coverlet up close to her chin. She had just closed her eyes when suddenly she heard a faint cry in the distance: "Lobster! Bloody back!"

Sarah knew immediately to whom the angry shouts were directed. Long bright red coats, white breeches, and three-cornered black hats were the uniform worn by the English soldiers.

The four thousand "redcoats," as they were sometimes called, had been stationed in Boston by King George III to patrol the city's sixteen thousand colonists. Boston and the rest of America still belonged to England. But the Turners and many other colonists were upset with England, believing they were unfairly denied representation in Parliament. They were called Whigs or Patriots. Colonists supportive of England's policies towards the colonies were known as Tories.

Sarah jumped out of bed and looked out the window. Boston's curfew had long since passed. The tower bells of Christ's Church had rung precisely at nine o'clock, signaling the townspeople to lock their doors and latch their shutters. The streets were empty, but Sarah could still hear the angry voices coming from somewhere in town.

She slipped her hooded cloak over her nightgown. Then she stepped into her leather shoes and wrapped her red scarf securely around her neck.

She opened the door of her bedchamber and peeked down the hall. Sarah's mother had made clear what punishment awaited her daughter if she were ever caught breaking curfew. Her mother would whip her bare feet with a birch rod until the soles of her feet turned as red as hot coals. While Sarah had never herself received a "trouncing," she had heard similar accounts from her friends.

The hall was quiet. With lantern in hand, Sarah sneaked down the stairs and into the dark coffee house. She unlatched the front door and peeked outside. The town crier had just walked by and was now headed south toward Long Wharf. In a raspy voice, he called out the time and weather as he paced the cobblestone street.

A dim light flickered from Sarah's lantern as she crept cautiously up King Street toward the Common. The shouts seemed to be coming from just a few blocks away. Curious, Sarah hurried along through the darkened, snow-covered street.

When she reached Boston's Town House, she saw a mob of colonists gathered at the steps of the Custom House. They were waving their lanterns and shouting at a group of soldiers standing at the entrance. Everyone was yelling at once, and all Sarah could make out were cries of "Bloody cowards!" and "Attack if you dare!" Sarah froze, unsure of what to do next.

Suddenly, someone from the crowd threw a snowball at one of the soldiers. Then another, and another. Soon, all that could be seen was a mass of flying snow and ice. Then someone hurled what looked like a large stick at another soldier, knocking his musket into the air. Sarah's heart quickened. Several men dove for the gun, but the soldier retrieved it immediately.

"Why don't you fire, you bloody redcoat!" shouted a man in the crowd. The mob erupted with more taunts and jeers. Sarah watched in horror as the soldier aimed his musket at the crowd.

All at once a shot rang out. Sarah gasped and ran toward the nearest building. Snow kicked up in her face as she pitched toward the ground. She crouched low against the side of the building and hid the lantern behind her long wool cloak. Her hand trembled, causing the pierced tin lantern to clank and rattle.

Sarah jumped as several more shots rang out. She cupped her hands over her ears and shut her eyes tightly. "Please, God, make them stop!"

Then, suddenly, an eerie silence fell over Boston. Sarah's body was taut as she listened. Gone were the echoes of gunfire and the shouts of rage. All was silent but for the soft crunch of fresh snow beneath her as she shifted position.

"ARM YOURSELVES!" shouted someone in the street. "GATHER YOUR MUSKETS AND BE PREPARED!"

The thunderous peal of church bells sounded all over Boston. And then, it seemed, from out of nowhere, men flocked onto King Street wielding shoulder guns and knives. Sarah knew they were the "minutemen," ready to fight in a minute's notice.

Gripping the lantern tightly in her hand, Sarah prepared to make an escape. She hiked up her cloak and with one leap darted out into the open like a hunted rabbit. She ran up King Street, heading straight for home. *Don't look back!* she told herself.

Bingham's Bookstore was a mere ten paces away when the commotion behind her reached a fevered pitch. She had to turn around just one more time.

Minutemen continued to pour into the street from every darkened corner, bearing torches and pumping their muskets defiantly into the air. "Captain Preston, show yourself!" several cried. But no redcoats appeared. Sarah wondered if the soldiers were lying in wait, preparing an ambush. She nervously eyed the trees and bushes around her.

Then Sarah saw several men being carried on the backs of some minutemen. *Were they dead?* She felt sick to her stomach. She had never been so scared in all her life.

Suddenly Sarah wished she had never left the safety of her bedchamber. She wanted to cry, but she couldn't. She was too frightened, too shocked by what she had seen. *How could she tell her parents about it? If they found out . . . no, she mustn't tell anyone.* Only her best friend, Hannah Adams, could be trusted.

9

The next morning, still shaky from her tension-filled night, Sarah learned the horrible news. "Your cousin Patrick was shot last night," said her father in a soft voice. "Doctor Boudineau said he lost too much blood . . . he's not expected to live."

Sarah sat stunned, unable to speak. *Patrick had been there last night?* If only she had known, perhaps she could have done something to help. She dropped her head in her hands and cried softly.

"I know how difficult this is for you, Sarah," Seth Turner said, wrapping his arm around her. "You two were like brother and sister." Her father's words only seemed to deepen her sadness.

Sarah recalled the day Patrick emigrated to Boston from Ireland three years ago. It seemed that from the moment he arrived, the two of them were inseparable. They did everything together. It was Patrick who taught her how to play "pickadill," a fierce game of chase in the snow. And it was Patrick who showed her how to clean fish and trap squirrels in the summer. Now, as she looked back, it seemed that they had squeezed an entire lifetime into such a short period of time. And for that, Sarah was grateful.

Sarah wiped her face with her apron. "What happened last night?" she asked finally.

Mr. Turner rose and moved to the hearth. His jaw tightened as he stared into the blazing logs.

"Patrick was there when a group of ropemakers got into an argument with some soldiers over the loss of odd jobs. It's no secret those bloody redcoats have been stealing work away from colonists just to fatten their pockets." Her father jabbed the sizzling coals with an iron poker. "No one is sure what happened next. All we know is that three of our men were killed on the spot."

Sarah's mother entered the room. Her tear-stained face was pallid and drawn. Her arms, strong and able for her tasks, hung limp next to her body. To Sarah, she suddenly looked fragile and much older than she actually was.

"I knew something like this would happen sooner or later," said her mother, closing her eyes. "Taking precious jobs away from men who can't even feed their families is pure greed. And Patrick—he was only twelve! How could they shoot an innocent boy?" Isabel Turner shook her head as tears slipped down her cheeks.

"Patrick told Dr. Boudineau that the soldiers had acted in self-defense. But I don't believe it," said her father, shaking his head. He rubbed his fingers across the deep creases in his brow. "Patrick has always been an exceptionally forgiving young man." He paused. Then looking at Sarah, he added, "Justice. That's all we can hope for now."

Sarah knew that justice could only prevail if

someone who saw what happened last night would come forward and testify. Otherwise, it would be the soldiers' word against that of the colonists.

Sarah shifted uncomfortably in her chair. She had been there. She knew she possessed the critical information that could help bring about justice for Patrick. But fear of what the soldiers might do once they heard her testimony chilled Sarah to the bone. *I can't testify,* she told herself. *I'll be declared an enemy to England—and who knows what they'll do to my parents!*

At first she was convinced that she had done the right thing by not telling anyone except Hannah. But when the trial came six months later, Sarah was shocked at the verdict: Captain Preston and all but two of the soldiers were set free. The other two were punished by having their thumbs branded with a hot iron—a mild punishment by most accounts. The Turners and many other Whigs agreed the trial was a terrible case of injustice. Many considered it yet another example of how England unfairly controlled their lives as colonists.

But for Sarah, the grief flowed much deeper. How her testimony could have changed the outcome of the trial, Sarah would never know. Not only had she let Patrick down, she had let herself down and everyone who was close to her as well.

Ever since that day, Sarah had never been the

same. The horrible memory of that night gnawed at her conscience from sunup to sundown. How she longed to make things right again. But how?

2

THE TEA ACT

"ARE YOU COMING, SARAH?" THE SHARP tone of her mother's voice snapped Sarah to attention. Sarah wondered how long she had been standing there at the woodpile holding the scarf.

"Yes, I'm coming, Mama," she called back. Quickly Sarah stuffed the scarf inside her apron. Then, holding out the apron's hem, she began loading firewood to carry inside.

Suddenly, Sarah felt a tap on her shoulder. She jumped, scattering the logs everywhere.

"It's only me, Sarah," said a cheery voice, giggling.

Sarah spun around. It was Hannah. She was wearing her mother's faded green bonnet. Her large blue eyes sparkled with amusement. It was obvious that Hannah derived great pleasure from scaring the daylights out of her dearest friend.

Sarah closed her eyes and sighed. "Oh, you are

wicked, Hannah," she said, managing a smile. "You gave me such a fright!"

Hannah cupped her hand over her mouth, trying not to laugh. "I didn't mean to frighten you, honestly. But you looked so serious, so deep in thought— I guess I couldn't help myself."

"I suppose not," said Sarah. She bent over and began picking up the logs. Hannah stooped to help her.

"Is something the matter, Sarah? You don't look well."

Sarah looked nervously over her shoulder. Then she leaned in toward Hannah. "Promise you won't tell?" she whispered.

"Promise."

Sarah reached into her apron and pulled out the scarf. She held it up to Hannah. "Recognize this?"

Hannah's forehead wrinkled as she studied the scarf. "No. Is it yours?"

"Yes. It's the scarf I wore on the night of the massacre, remember?"

"Oh, yes, now I do. But I thought you had lost it."

"I had," said Sarah. "But when I came out to the woodpile this morning I found it folded neatly on top of the firewood."

"How strange. Do you think someone just found it and is returning it to you?"

"No," said Sarah, shaking her head. "Look at it. It

is as neat and clean as the day I lost it. Someone had to have taken care of it all this time. Anyway, why wouldn't it have been returned sooner? And why not hand it to me in person?"

Hannah shrugged her shoulders.

Sarah looked down at the scarf. "Whoever put this here obviously wanted me to find it. But why? Is someone trying to tell me something?"

"I don't know," said Hannah, folding her arms tightly across her chest. "It all sounds a bit strange to me. Will you tell your parents?"

"Never," answered Sarah sharply. "If I tell them about the scarf, then I'll have to tell them about the night I lost it. And I have no wish to do that—not after all this time."

"Saaarahhhh!"

Isabel Turner stood at the back door of the coffee house. Her right hand gripped the top of a broom. The other rested firmly on her hip. She did not look pleased. "If those coals have already turned black, you'll have to fetch the hearth shovel, for you'll be begging the neighbors for hot coals. Is that clear?"

"Yes, ma'am!"

This time Mrs. Turner stood guard at the door, eyeing her daughter. A cold silence followed as Sarah went about her work dutifully, loading as many logs into her apron as she could carry.

As they walked in the back door, Sarah heard a familiar voice coming from the coffee shop. It was Hannah's father, Samuel Adams.

"I only hope the colonists will not bow to the pressure," Sarah heard him say. Mr. Adams was a close friend to her father and an important leader among the Whigs, although no one would know it by his appearance. No matter how much his wife, Betsy, fussed over his clothes, they never looked neat. He wore the same shabby red coat every day, and Sarah wondered if he had ever owned a comb in his life. As a child she used to imagine what she might find inside that mass of tangled hair. Even his wigs, when he chose to wear them, looked as if he had slept in them the night before.

Although Mr. Adams was now regarded by many as a great leader, Sarah knew his troubled past— how he had squandered his father's inheritance and had failed miserably in business. But what baffled Sarah most was observing how he handled these disappointments. He couldn't have cared less what people said about him. Instead, he discovered what his true talents were and then, with great passion, pursued them.

Samuel Adams now spent most of his time writing newspaper articles urging people to stand up for their rights against England. His faithful perseverance inspired Sarah.

Broom in hand, Mrs. Turner followed close behind the girls, whisking away whatever traces of dirt they had tracked inside. "Hurry along with the wood," she demanded. "We must warm up the room before we open for business."

Hannah helped Sarah carry the logs to the huge brick fireplace inside the coffee house. Ten small, round oak tables, each with five high-backed chairs, filled the long, narrow room. The air was sweet with the scent of beeswax candles centered on every table.

Sarah felt her cheeks flush when she saw Hannah's older brother, Sam Jr. He was seated at a table with her father, Mr. Adams, and Mr. Charles Hendricks, another Whig and close friend of Mr. Adams. Mr. Hendricks, a quiet, private man, turned to Sarah and smiled politely.

That funny feeling in Sarah's stomach that surfaced whenever Sam was around was back again. *Surely it would pass, whatever it was.*

Sam stood up when he saw Sarah enter the room. He was rugged and tall and looked handsome in his gray waistcoat and white vest. "Let me help you with that, Miss Turner," he said.

Lately Sarah had found herself thinking of excuses to go to Hannah's house so she could spy on Sam. Oftentimes she would find him sitting at the Adams's kitchen table talking with his father about the latest news from England. He was an honest young man, and smart, too. After graduating from school three years ago at the age of thirteen, he had planned to continue his education, perhaps at Harvard, but the Adamses lacked the funds to send him.

Sam knelt down on the hearth and stacked several logs inside the fireplace. Then he fed small branches to the glowing embers until they flamed once again. "There you are," he said, gazing up at Sarah. "This fire will chase out the cold soon enough."

Sarah's eyes met Sam's for a brief moment. She smiled, and then quickly looked down and smoothed out her apron.

"Charles and I agree, Seth, that we should prepare for greater opposition from the Tories now that King George has passed this new law," said Mr. Adams.

Sarah knew what Mr. Adams was speaking about. News of the Tea Act had many colonists worried about their economic future. British Parliament had passed the law in May. But it wasn't the first time England had passed a law concerning tea. British tea had become a popular drink among the colonists, and England knew it. Almost every man, woman, and child consumed British tea every day. It was sold in the coffee house along with other beverages, including coffee, cider, ale, and alcoholic punches—that is, it had been sold until six years ago when Parliament slapped a three-pence-a-pound tax on the popular potion.

To fight the tax, Sarah's father encouraged his customers and other shopkeepers to refuse to buy and sell British tea and other taxed goods from England. He called it a *boycott*—a means of pressuring England to remove the tax on these goods.

Rather than selling British tea, Sarah's father sold the less expensive Dutch tea. It was more bitter-tasting than the British variety, and selling it was risky business because the tea had to be smuggled in from Holland. But Sarah's father and others believed that England shouldn't tax the colonies without allowing them to be represented in Parliament. "Taxation without representation," he called it. Most colonists agreed and went along with the boycott.

But now the situation had changed dramatically. The Tea Act lowered the price of the British tea below that of the smuggled Dutch tea. Sarah feared that people would give in to England's scheme and buy the taxed tea. She worried about the impact it would have on the family business if people stopped buying their Dutch tea.

The Tea Act also provided that England would now choose which merchants would be authorized to sell their tea within the colony. These merchants, or tea agents, included Governor Thomas Hutchinson and Mr. Richard Clarke, both of whom were wealthy and well-known Tories in Boston. *It isn't right,* Sarah had lamented. *King George is trying to drive Papa out of business just because he's a Whig.*

Mr. Hendricks sat up straight in his chair and cleared his throat. "Seth," he said, his gray eyes staring intently, "the Tories aren't going to like you stirring up trouble against the Tea Act by encouraging others to support the boycott."

"I'm sure you're right, Charles," said Sarah's father. "But we must continue to fight against these unfair taxes or England will sense that we're giving up and will tax us even more. First the tax on tea, then what? If England keeps taxing other common goods, we'll all surely suffer—some more than others."

Sarah looked at her father. What did he mean by "some more than others"? *Is he talking about us?*

"I couldn't agree more," said Mr. Adams. He rose from the table and smoothed his fingers along the brim of his tri-cornered hat. "Well, we best be going."

Sarah's father stood up and shook hands with the three men. "I certainly appreciate your coming by."

"We just wish we had better news for you, Seth,"

said Mr. Adams.

Sam turned to tip his hat to Sarah. "Good day, Miss Turner."

Sarah acknowledged him with a gracious nod. Turning to Hannah, she whispered, "I wish you didn't have to go."

"Don't fret about the scarf," Hannah whispered back. "I'm sure you'll figure it out soon enough."

Sarah smiled weakly.

But as she waved to Hannah through the shop window, she had an uneasy feeling that something terrible was about to happen.

3

AN ANONYMOUS NOTE

THE NEXT MORNING SARAH AWOKE EARLY. She was anxious to see what, if anything, the mysterious person had left for her out on the woodpile.

Her eyes burned, a reminder of the hours she had tossed and turned during the night. She reached for her hoop petticoat and stay hanging from the wooden hooks attached to her chamber wall. Stays were wood-framed undergarments, like corsets, worn by ladies to help them stand straight. Sarah found them so dreadful that she once suggested to Hannah that prisoners be forced to wear them as a form of torture. Together they made a pact, vowing never to make their own children wear them.

Next she donned a long-sleeved sage-and-cream-colored linen dress. She fastened the buttons quickly and pulled a fresh apron over the dress. Her long auburn hair was piled high on her head and covered with a clean muslin cap.

Sarah dashed down the stairs, unaware of her apron's sash, still untied, whipping the air behind her.

"Where are you off to in such a hurry?" asked her mother.

"Hoping to get an early start on my chores, that's all."

Sarah's mother eyed her daughter suspiciously. "'Hoping to get an early start on my chores'?" repeated her mother. Even Sarah didn't think it sounded believable.

Without stopping to explain, Sarah bustled past her mother and burst through the back door. Strangely, she was almost hoping there would be something there, something that would give her another clue to the scarf mystery. Could it somehow be tied to all the talk of the Tea Act? After all, the Whigs hadn't been this angry since the massacre three years ago.

Her heart began pounding with excitement as she broke into a slow trot toward the woodpile. As she came closer, though, all she could see was a tidy heap of logs.

Maybe Hannah was right, she thought. *Maybe someone did find the scarf after all this time and is returning it to the rightful owner, and nothing more.*

She breathed deeply. The best course of action now, she decided, was to put the entire incident behind her. After all, there was plenty to worry about with the Tea Act.

By early afternoon, the coffee house was packed full of customers. The handbills posted in town had listed the names of the tea agents England had chosen—all Tories, of course. The news angered the Whigs, many of whom had gathered at the coffee house to complain.

Sarah was everywhere, taking orders, pouring cider, brewing coffee, serving food, mopping up spills, greeting customers, and counting money. Even with her parents' help, there were not enough hands to manage the crowd.

"Don't worry, Seth," Sarah heard Mr. Bennett say. "England can't buy our allegiance by lowering the price of its tea, no, sir! We'll continue to support the boycott. You can count on us!"

It pleased Sarah to see so much support. There was strength in unity and Sarah knew it.

By late afternoon, the crowds had died down to a manageable few. "We're running low on soap, Sarah," her mother noted. "'Tis a fine time to make more before business picks up again."

Sarah's legs ached from fatigue as she walked slowly to the hearth to collect ashes for the soap. *At least we don't have to rely on England for our*

soap, she muttered to herself.

She carried the ashes behind the coffee house, where she dumped them into a large, wooden, box-like structure her father had built. First, she poured water slowly over the ashes. The resulting liquid, called lye, dripped through small holes and into a pan Sarah had placed underneath.

She removed the pan and mixed in the animal lard her mother had set aside in a wooden bowl. She stuck her thumb in the mixture to test for proper thickness. "It must be thick enough to float an egg," her mother once said.

After she worked to perfect the soft, gooey soap, she collected her things to go back inside. As she turned to leave, a cold numbness gripped her. From the corner of her eye, she noticed a small object lying atop the woodpile.

She walked closer. It was a scroll of fine Dutch paper tied with a red ribbon—the same kind that had been tied around the scarf. Sarah's heart skipped a beat. That shade of red was like a warning sign, signaling danger.

Sarah reached out and grabbed the note. She pulled the ribbon at one end, loosening the neatly tied bow. With trembling fingers, she unrolled the paper and stared at the words printed in black ink.

She read the first sentence: *I saw you that night, March 5, 1770.* She stopped, unable to breathe. Her eyes dropped to the bottom of the note. There was no signature, no name. She blinked her eyes and read the sentence again, this time more slowly. *I—saw—you—that—night,—March—5,—1770.*

The words pierced her like a razor-sharp knife. She read on: *You think no one saw you, but I did. You saw what happened but refused to come forward at the trial. If this gets out, you and your family will be ruined! So tell your father to stop stirring up trouble or else.*

Sarah stood statue-still with her shoulders hunched. She clutched the note against her chest. Through the thin paper she could feel her heart pounding wildly. Each rhythmic pulse made the paper beat in time as if it were alive, calling forth the haunting words, *You and your family will be ruined . . . ruined . . . ruined!*

"Sarah!"

Her mother's distant shout snapped Sarah to as she spun around. "Yes, Mama?"

"What's wrong with you, young lady? That's the third time I called you." Sarah said nothing. Her mother shook her head. "You have a visitor."

A visitor? The only person who came to see her was Hannah. But Hannah wouldn't bother asking for Sarah; she'd simply search the entire coffee house by herself until she found her.

"It's Laura Potter. She's here with her mother."

Sarah made a face. "Laura wants to see *me*?"

"Yes. Mrs. Potter dropped by to tell me how Mrs. Harrison's ankle is mending from her spill last week. They were just about to leave when Laura asked for you."

When her mother turned away, Sarah tucked the note inside her sleeve and walked, unhurried, to the back door of the coffee house.

Inside the shop's kitchen, Sarah found her mother busy at work stirring the contents of a brass kettle hanging from an iron crane inside the fireplace. Sarah plunged her hands into a basin of cold water and slowly dried them off, one finger at a time. The longer Laura had to wait, the better.

"Stop dawdling away the hours," ordered her mother as she looked over her shoulder. She swung the kettle back into the fireplace with a sudden jerk. "Laura and her mother are waiting."

Laura Potter was known as a troublemaker who seemed to have more money than friends. Considering that Laura's father was known as one of Boston's finest physicians, Sarah found it amusing that Dr. Potter worked to ease people's suffering while his daughter enjoyed causing it.

Sarah saw Laura and her mother standing near the front door of the Maple Leaf. As usual, Laura was robed in the latest fashion. Her fine, silk dress, the color of a robin's egg, had rich lace detailing throughout. *Probably one of those fancy London imports,* grumbled Sarah to herself. Her blond hair was swept up in a delicate twist with just the right hat to complement her dress.

Laura flashed a civil grin and Mrs. Potter nodded as Sarah approached them. "So kind of you to interrupt your busy day, Miss Sarah," said Mrs. Potter. Her face was pink and her expression strained. Sarah wondered if her ivory stays were tied too tight around her thick waist.

"Indeed," said Laura. She glanced down at Sarah's filthy apron with a disapproving look. "You don't look well, dear Sarah."

"I'm fine," said Sarah, lying. The smug expression on Laura's face told Sarah she was up to no good. Suddenly, Sarah noticed the tip of a red ribbon hanging just below Laura's hat. She thought about the red ribbon tied around the note still tucked inside her sleeve. *Could Laura have placed the note? No, that's pure folly. I'm just being foolish,* she reasoned.

"So, what have you been up to these days, Sarah? Anything, um, *new*?" Laura gave Sarah a mischievous grin as she stared into her eyes.

Sarah's posture stiffened. "New? What exactly do you mean?"

Laura chuckled. "Oh, nothing. You just look a bit, let's say, preoccupied, that's all."

Sarah stared at Laura. *Could she be referring to the scarf—or maybe the note she had found just moments ago?* The idea wasn't so far-fetched, really. Laura would love nothing more than to discover a terrible secret in Sarah's past.

Finally, Mrs. Potter broke the silence. She looked at Sarah and smiled, causing a dark mole on her cheek to protrude slightly. "We heard about the new law—the Tea Act, I think they call it. We know how outspoken your father is about the tax. We're just concerned for you and your family." Mrs. Potter turned to her daughter. "That is what you meant to say, isn't it, dear?"

Laura smirked. "Indeed. It would be such a shame to see your family suffer because of your father's political views."

Sarah could feel her face grow hot. "My father—that is, our family—is going to be just fine. You needn't worry about us!" And with that, Sarah turned and stormed through the door leading to the kitchen.

Up the stairs she bounded, then turned sharply into her bedchamber, slamming the door behind her. With one flying leap, she landed stomach-first onto her bed.

She closed her eyes and replayed the scene with Laura and Mrs. Potter in her mind. She pictured Laura's spiteful grin and how she seemed to be enjoying her little game with Sarah. *What a miserable sort she is,* thought Sarah. *Is this just another one of her dreadful tricks? Does she know anything at all?*

Sarah stopped when she heard someone stomping up the stairs. She sat upright on her bed as the door burst open.

"What in heaven's name do you think you're doing, child?" cried her mother. "Everyone in Boston heard that door slam! And what about the way you spoke to Mrs. Potter and her daughter—in front of our customers, no less!"

"I'm sorry, Mama," said Sarah. "It's just that Laura is a terrible snob who never has anything good to say about—"

"Never you mind!" scolded her mother. "Don't you recall what your father taught you about how to behave in front of our customers?" Sarah dropped her head, knowing she had already lost the argument.

"Sarah, we cannot afford to lose any business because of your rude behavior." Mrs. Turner closed her eyes and shook her head. "Lord knows I've done my best to try to raise you like a proper lady, but you have a mind of your own, Sarah. I ought to give you a good thrashing right now!"

"Mama, I—" Sarah stopped.

"Well, what is it, child?"

Sarah wanted to tell her all about the scarf and the note and how nasty Laura had acted toward her. But it was no use. Telling her mother now would only upset her more.

"I'm sorry," said Sarah quietly. "I won't let it happen again."

"See that you don't."

4

TWELVE STITCHES TO THE INCH

"**L**ET'S GO, SARAH, OR WE'LL BE LATE FOR the quilting," called her mother from the hallway. "I don't want to keep Mrs. Adams and the others waiting."

"I'm coming, Mama."

Mrs. Turner's mouth dropped open when she entered Sarah's bedchamber. "Goodness gracious, child!"

Sarah was bent over, elbow-deep in her hope chest. Ribbons, partly finished needlework, and other keepsakes were flying over her head.

"I can't seem to find my sewing needle," muttered Sarah. "I know it's in here somewhere."

Her mother left the room briefly and then returned with one of her own needles. "Here," she said, holding it out to Sarah. "You can borrow one of mine for now."

Sarah pulled her shawl tightly around her

shoulders as she walked with her mother to the small, run-down house on Purchase Street. It was a cool, crisp November day. Brown and gold leaves whirled and danced everywhere.

It had been four weeks since Sarah had discovered the red scarf and the anonymous note. But the threat against her family was still fresh in her mind.

Sarah had tried on several occasions to talk to her father about the note. But the time never seemed right. If he wasn't working in the coffee house, he was meeting with his fellow Whigs to discuss strategy. And from the tired look in his eyes, Sarah knew that the stress of it all was beginning to take its toll.

"Mama," said Sarah as they turned the corner, "do you think the boycott is going to work?"

"I don't know, Sarah," her mother answered softly. "Your father is a mite worried that people are beginning to soften their stand on the tea tax."

"But what about all those people who told us they'd support us and continue to buy smuggled tea instead of British tea? Don't they care anymore?"

Mrs. Turner stopped. She turned and looked her daughter in the eye. "They may want to support the boycott, but money is tight and some people can't afford the higher-priced Dutch tea. That's just the way it is."

Sarah could see the worry in her mother's eyes. She wished her mother would talk to her. *Really* talk to her. It seemed to Sarah that mothers were always covering up for the sake of their children. Hannah agreed, and together they'd made another pact that when they became mothers, they wouldn't play such foolish games with their children.

Sarah looked up toward the Adams's house. Mr. Adams and Mr. Hendricks were walking out together. Sarah's mother elbowed her daughter. "Look cheerful," she whispered.

"Good afternoon, ladies," said Mr. Adams. Both men tipped their hats in gentlemanly fashion.

"I'm sure my wife will be pleased to see you both were able to join in on the quilt," said Mr. Adams.

"Indeed," added Mr. Hendricks. "I believe she has enough work inside to keep you busy straight through afternoon tea."

Sarah's mother smiled knowingly. "In that case, we mustn't keep Mrs. Adams waiting. Good day to you both."

Betsy Adams was at the door to greet them when they arrived. "Well, if it isn't young Miss Turner and her lovely mother. It's so good of you both to come. Do make yourselves at home."

A pleasing aroma of apples and cinnamon wafted through the air as they entered the foyer. Lively chatter seeped in from the adjoining room.

Sarah looked around at the familiar surroundings. The humble furnishings in the Adams's home always had a calm, soothing effect on her. There was something about the small cozy rooms, lumpy seat cushions, and simple embroidered patterns on the pillows that made Sarah feel at home.

After taking their cloaks, Mrs. Adams led them into the parlor, where a few women were already seated.

Sarah looked around the room. She stiffened. There, sitting at the far end of the room, were Laura Potter and her mother. Mrs. Potter waved at Sarah with her pinky finger and Sarah waved back. Laura smirked as she raised her cup to her mouth.

Then, without warning, Laura sneezed violently, spilling hot cider down the front of her silk dress. When she looked down and saw the dark stain, Laura let out such a shriek that Sarah thought she had sat on her sewing needle. Mrs. Potter tried to blot the stain with her lace handkerchief, but Laura fussed and pushed her hand away. Sarah bit her lip to keep from laughing.

Sarah's mother darted across the room to chat with Mrs. Otis. At eighty-seven, Mrs. Otis was the oldest citizen in Boston, and a proud Whig at that.

"Hannah's in the kitchen pouring hot apple cider, Sarah," said Mrs. Adams. "We'll be getting started as soon as the others arrive."

* * * * *

The quilt was magnificent. It was attached with twine to a large quilting frame held up by four chairs, stretched out like a tabletop in the center of the room.

Sarah pulled up her chair close to the frame and surveyed the artwork. Stars of varying sizes and distinctive geometric designs graced the cover of the quilt. Brilliant colors of sky blue, emerald green, and strawberry red made the shapes appear to pop out against the creamy white background. It was one of the most beautiful things Sarah had ever seen.

Hannah eased into the chair next to Sarah.

"Oh, it's truly beautiful," said Sarah, spellbound.

Hannah's face was ashen as she leaned toward Sarah. "Follow me into the kitchen," she whispered in a jittery voice. "I have something I have to give you."

"What is it?"

"Come and I'll show you."

Sarah followed Hannah into the kitchen. With a hesitant hand, Hannah produced a scroll of paper with a red ribbon tied around it. It looked just like the one Sarah had found on the woodpile. But this note had Sarah's name printed in small letters on the outside.

"I found this on one of the chairs in the parlor

just before you came in," said Hannah.

Sarah opened the note. Her voice was steady as she read it out loud: *"I see that you and your father have chosen to ignore my note—a most unwise decision. Perhaps you think this is merely a foolish prank. Think again!"*

"Oh, Sarah!" cried Hannah. "Who do you think would write such a dreadful thing?"

"It must be Laura," said Sarah emphatically. "Think about it. You said you found the note in the room just moments before I arrived." Hannah nodded. "And there were only three women present: Laura, her mother, and Mrs. Otis. And we know it can't be Mrs. Otis. Her hand is too unsteady to write such a note."

"So what do you do now?"

"Nothing."

"Nothing?"

"If Laura saw me that night," said Sarah, "that means she was there, too. So why didn't she come forward at the trial? For the same reason I didn't — she was too scared."

"You're right," said Hannah. "Maybe these threats *are* hollow."

"Precisely," said Sarah. "She can't expose me without revealing that she was there that night, too."

"But why is she doing this in the first place?"

"I don't know," said Sarah. "Maybe she enjoys

41

watching me squirm. In any case, it's best if I act like nothing's wrong. Maybe that way she'll tire of this silly game and leave me alone."

Hannah and Sarah rejoined the group. There were now twelve ladies gathered around the quilt. Everyone listened intently as Betsy explained the pattern everyone was to follow.

"I know one thing," whispered Hannah slyly. "I can sew faster and better than you can."

Sarah smiled, grateful to her friend for trying to break the tension. "You think, huh?"

"It's true," said Hannah. "At least I finished the needlepoint pillow I started last year. You have so many unfinished projects, you could patch them all together and make your very first quilt." It was true. Sarah always found her reading more satisfying than her needlepoint.

They both giggled as they began pulling their needles through the cotton fabric. It felt good to laugh, especially now that Sarah had figured out Laura's scheme. It was as if a huge weight had been lifted from Sarah's shoulders. Now she could relax.

Sarah concentrated on making small, even stitches. "Twelve stitches to the inch," her mother had reminded her repeatedly. Sarah preferred to think of the measurement as a goal—something to strive for as one became more experienced. Surely her mother didn't mean *every* inch.

When the last stitch was finally secured in place, everyone stood back and admired the collective handiwork. It was indeed an exquisite piece. It had been two-and-a-half hours since they started, and suddenly Sarah could feel every stitch in her fingers.

That night, as Sarah lay awake in bed, she thought about Laura and the notes and everything that had happened over the last month. Although she was convinced that Laura had planted the notes, there was one thing that still bothered her. *Why had Laura waited three years to plant the scarf? Why hadn't she done something before?*

5

THE TEA SHIPS

THE SUN WAS WARM ON SARAH'S FACE AS she washed the windows in front of the Maple Leaf. Cool water dripped down the inside of her sleeve as she reached for the upper panes.

Through the glass, Sarah saw a crowd of people gathered around a tree in front of Bingham's Bookstore just across the street. Sarah set down her rag and walked over to see what the commotion was all about.

There was a sign posted on the tree. The note read:

Ladies and Gentlemen:
There is a town meeting today at noon at the Liberty Tree. We will ask the tea agents to stop selling England's tea and to return the tea ships.

Sarah rushed back to tell her parents. "Maybe

this is what we've been waiting for, Papa," she said excitedly. "If we can force the tea back to England, King George will know we mean business."

"Don't get your hopes up," her father warned. "The tea agents are probably too scared of England to listen to us."

Just before noon, the town crier rang a copper bell and shouted, "HEAR YE! HEAR YE! MEETING AT THE LIBERTY TREE!"

Sarah helped her father lock up the coffee house. Together they walked to Hanover Square, where the hundred-year-old elm called "The Liberty Tree" stood.

A crowd twenty people deep had already gathered by the time they arrived. At exactly noon, Samuel Adams started the meeting.

"My fellow countrymen, as you can see, the agents have made their position quite clear by refusing to appear before us today."

The crowd erupted with angry shouts: "Cowards!" "Turncoats!" "Traitors!"

Mr. Adams held up his hand to silence the crowd. "Since they have refused our invitation, I say we shall pay them a surprise visit!"

"YES! YES!"

"We know the agents' whereabouts even as we speak. A group of us shall confront them and demand they resign as tea agents. We shall also demand that they send the expected tea shipments back to England as soon as they reach Boston.

"Let us not waver in our attempt to remain loyal to this most noble of endeavors. Levying taxes, even a single farthing, against us without our consent is pure extortion!"

With a final cheer, the crowds dispersed. Sarah's eyes were bright with hope as she walked beside her father back to the coffee house. She smiled as she recalled Mr. Adams's final words: *Levying taxes, even a single farthing, against us without our consent is pure extortion!*

Sarah's father reached out to open the door to the coffee house when he stopped suddenly. "What's this?" he asked.

Sarah went rigid with shock. A third note, scrolled up with a red ribbon, was wedged into the door of the Maple Leaf. Again, there was writing on the outside. This time, however, there were only four letters: S-E-T-H.

Sarah was stunned. *Why would Laura address a note to her father? Was she really that intent on destroying Sarah? Why?* Suddenly, nothing seemed to make sense.

Terrified, Sarah watched as her father slid the ribbon off the paper. She knew that within moments, her entire world could shatter. The worst part was knowing that her father would hear about

the night of the massacre not from her but from an anonymous source. At least she owed her father the decency of hearing it from her own lips, even if it were three years late.

Sarah opened her mouth, ready to confess everything right there on King Street in broad daylight. But something made her stop.

She studied his face as he opened the paper and began reading the note. She followed his eyes as they scanned each line.

"What does it say?" she asked, afraid to know the answer.

With one hand he crumpled up the paper and stuffed it into his waistcoat. He looked at his daughter. "You needn't worry about it, Sarah."

"No, I . . . I really want to know," she pleaded.

He hesitated. Then he said, "Someone has threatened to run us out of business if I continue to resist the Tea Act." He shook his head in disbelief. "Must be some Tory thinking he can scare me with a little piece of paper. He must take me a fool!"

Sarah breathed a sigh of relief. *At least there was no mention of her. But why would Laura now involve her father? And why was he convinced that a Tory wrote the note? Could she have been wrong about Laura all this time?* All the clues—the visit in the coffee house, the ribbon in Laura's hair, the note at the quilting party—they all pointed to Laura.

"Papa," she asked, "do you think this person is serious about her—I mean, *his*—threat?"

"He might be serious, but what can he do to us?"

Silence followed. Only Sarah knew the real answer to that question.

"Don't fret, Sarah," said her father, gently patting her shoulder. "There's nothing to worry about. Mr. Adams and Mr. Hendricks had predicted as much. Anytime you take a stand on something important, you're going to experience resistance. It's perfectly normal."

Sarah didn't feel perfectly normal. She felt perfectly horrible! The truth was that if she *had* taken a stand on behalf of Patrick, there wouldn't be all this resistance in the first place.

Later that day, Sarah overheard her father talking to Mr. Adams at the Maple Leaf. "The tea agents refused our request," said Mr. Adams. "They claim they lack authority from England to comply with our demands."

"That's foolishness!" cried her father. "Don't they fear the townspeople will retaliate?"

"I'm sure they do. But they're even more frightened of disobeying King George."

"There must be another way," said her father. "We simply cannot allow the tea ships to land in Boston Harbor!"

*   *   *   *   *

A brisk November wind made Sarah's eyes tear as she walked with her parents to Sunday services. The crisp air carried the scent of salt water and the first catch of the day. Sarah gently closed her watery eyes and took a deep breath. Suddenly her drowsy senses became alert when she heard a man call out as he ran up the street: "DON'T LET THEM LAND!"

At once, Sarah's father took off running toward the wharf. Despite her mother's protest, Sarah dropped her Bible and ran after him.

When they arrived, one of the dockworkers filled them in. The British ship *Dartmouth* had been sighted out at sea. It was projected to reach Boston the next day. And over one hundred tea chests were expected to be on board.

"We must send back the tea! We must!" someone shouted behind her.

Later that afternoon, Sarah learned from Mr. Adams that the *Dartmouth* and two other tea ships, the *Eleanor* and the *Beaver,* were expected to arrive in Boston later that week.

"What are we going to do, Papa?" Sarah asked her father. "Mr. Adams said that the tea agents have refused to send back the ships. And we cannot hold the ships in Boston forever."

"I'll soon find out. There's a gathering tonight at

the Old South Meeting House."

"May I go, Papa?"

"I'm sorry, Sarah. Only men are allowed."

Men only. It made no sense to Sarah. Besides, she couldn't count on the handbills posted around town to carry the full story. They never did. This meeting would be important for the future of her family and all of Boston. Somehow she had to attend, but how?

Then she had an idea. She looked out the window. The sun was beginning to dip behind the storefronts. There wasn't much time.

6

A NARROW ESCAPE

"MAMA," CALLED SARAH FROM THE kitchen doorway. "These gloves belong to Hannah. I must return them. May I go now?" Sarah clutched the gloves in her hands. She hoped her mother wouldn't ask to see them. The cream-colored gloves were now soiled with deep creases throughout, a telling sign of the countless months they had spent in the bottom of Sarah's blanket chest.

Her mother glanced at the unfamiliar objects. "It's getting late, Sarah. Soon it will be dark as pitch. Must you go now?"

Sarah was quick to answer. "Oh, yes, Mama. With the weather turning frightfully cold, I wouldn't want Hannah to suffer."

Isabel Turner eyed her daughter. Sarah looked away, averting her mother's penetrating gaze. She prayed her mother wouldn't ask any more questions.

Finally her mother answered. "You may go, but mind you don't stay too—" But Sarah had already dashed out the door.

She ran all the way to Hannah's house. From the road, Sarah could see the faint glow of a candle flicker through Hannah's chamber window. She tapped on the glass and waited for Hannah to appear.

Hannah smiled when she saw Sarah. She opened the window and poked her head outside. "Fancy to see you here."

"I don't have time to talk," said Sarah, panting. "Here. Take these gloves." Sarah ran off before Hannah could speak. "I'll tell you all about it tomorrow," Sarah called behind her.

She ran on through the streets of Boston, taking her favorite shortcuts. Darkness was falling quickly. In her haste, Sarah had forgotten her lantern. *Just as well,* she thought. *The light would only bring attention my way.*

As she turned onto Washington Street, she could see the grand steeple of the Old South Meeting House. Sarah fetched a barrel from the candle shop next door and rolled it up to one of the church's tall, narrow windows. She stood on the barrel and peered through the glass.

Many Boston men, all of them Whigs, filled the high-walled box pews. Every eye was fixed up front on the man in the familiar shabby red waistcoat. Sarah leaned closer to search for her father. Seeing was difficult; the glass fogged with every breath. She covered her mouth and wiped the glass.

Finally, she spotted her father seated in the second box next to Mr. Hendricks and Sam Jr. Everyone, including her father, was too engrossed to notice her at the window.

Sarah stood perfectly still and strained to hear Mr. Adams. "We must devise a new plan," he said. "We've met with the tea agents and the ship captains. Both refuse to return the tea to England."

"Let's destroy the tea!" shouted a man sitting just three feet from Sarah's window. Everyone turned toward him and cheered loudly. Sarah ducked. She wondered if her father—or worse, Sam—had noticed her.

"Interesting idea," agreed Mr. Adams. "Just one important point. We must remain anonymous, for anyone caught in our scheme will surely be arrested."

Sarah raised her head again slowly and looked. Mr. Adams was pacing in front of the church. "We need ideas on how to destroy the tea and, at the same time, protect the men involved."

"Set it on fire in the middle of the night!" shouted a large man with a raised fist.

Mr. Adams rubbed his stubbly chin with the back of his hand. "Maybe, but that could get dan-

gerous. I say we take no unnecessary risks. Any other ideas?"

After a few moments, Mr. Parker, who owned the glass shop on Market Street, stood up and faced the group. Sarah knew Mr. Parker as a thoughtful man with keen insight. He was so soft-spoken, however, that Sarah found it difficult to hear him through the glass.

She leaned in closer. "—throw the tea into the—" Sarah could see Mr. Parker's lips still moving, but his voice trailed off. A man sitting in a box near her window turned to the man next to him and said, "That'll be one heck of a tea party!"

Just then, Sarah's heel caught the rim of the barrel. Her knee buckled beneath her, tossing her sideways onto the cold, hard ground. The barrel made a terrific crashing sound as it smashed into the side of the building.

"Who goes there?" shouted a man's voice from the rear of the church.

Sarah froze. There in the black shadows of the church, she closed her eyes and listened. A gentle breeze rustled the leaves behind her. Then she heard a soft padding sound coming from somewhere in the distance. *Where was the man? What would she say if he confronted her?*

After several tense moments, Sarah heard the creak of rusty door hinges near the rear of the building. Then there was a loud bang as the door slammed shut.

Sarah waited a while longer to make sure it was safe to move. Finally, she leaned forward and peered out from the side of the building. The man was gone.

7

THE DISCOVERY

NO ONE NEEDED TO WAKE SARAH THE NEXT morning. Her ankle throbbed from last night's fall, keeping her up most of the night. The scene at the church had been a close call, but Sarah was glad she had gone. At least now she knew that Mr. Adams and the others were brewing a plan to destroy the tea.

She dressed quickly and hobbled down the stairs, favoring her sore ankle. When she reached the bottom step, she was surprised to hear male voices coming from inside the coffee house. She knew they couldn't be customers; the shop would not be open until midday.

The door leading to the coffee house suddenly swung open, startling Sarah. "Good morning, dear," said her mother cheerfully. "I'm glad you're up. Your father and Mr. Adams are meeting with a few men in the shop to discuss some important matters.

I'd like you to serve them coffee and biscuits while I begin roasting turkey and making pumpkin cake to serve our customers this afternoon."

Sarah nodded. It wasn't the first time the Whigs had used the coffee house for secret meetings. The Maple Leaf's central location in town made it a convenient place to meet in private.

Mr. Adams abruptly stopped talking when Sarah opened the door. All five men gathered around the small oak table glanced up at her. They immediately turned back to Mr. Adams, however, when they saw that it was only her.

"It's agreed then," continued Mr. Adams. "We will choose a group of men. On the evening of December 16th, they will board the ships disguised as Mohawk Indians and dump the tea chests into the harbor."

Sarah could hardly believe what she was hearing. *Men dressed as Indians destroying England's precious tea . . . it was perfect!*

She smiled as she walked quickly to the back of the shop and placed the day-old biscuits on the gridiron. She held the gridiron over the fire until the biscuits were warm.

With a kettle of coffee in one hand and the plate of biscuits in the other, Sarah hurried back to their table.

"We must remember one thing," said her father,

as Sarah poured steaming coffee into the pewter mugs her mother had set on the table. "Only those involved need to know of our plan. One small leak and the entire operation could fail."

"Indeed," agreed Mr. Hendricks. "We must keep this a secret."

As the deadline of December 16th approached, Sarah wondered if she were the only girl in Boston who knew of the plan to dump the tea overboard. The thought made her feel important and anxious at the same time. Some days, Sarah's stomach would twist in knots at the knowledge that her father would be one of the "Indians" who would be there that night facing possible danger. Other days, she was filled with confidence, certain that everything would go well.

But destroying tea was not the only thing on Sarah's mind. Over the past two weeks, she had given much thought to the identity of the mystery writer. She no longer believed it was Laura—the last note to her father had convinced her of that. It had to be someone as interested in the Tea Act as in what had happened three years ago. But who?

Just past midday on December 15th, Sarah slipped on her hooded cloak and headed to Hannah's house to see what, if anything, Hannah knew of tomorrow's plan.

As she rounded the corner onto Purchase Street, Sarah saw Mr. Hendricks walking out of the Adams's house. He appeared deep in thought and walked at a deliberate pace. Then, as he turned up King Street, Sarah noticed something fall from his waistcoat. She called out for him, but her voice was lost in the screeching cry of the seagulls overhead.

She ran up the path. *It could be something important,* she told herself. *If I hurry, maybe I can return it to him before he's too far away.*

The morning sun had seared through the snow, revealing the wet cobblestones underneath. Her eyes searched the rocky pavement as it glistened in the sun. Then, what she saw just off the road made her stop dead in her tracks. For there, amidst a patch of dying grass, was a single red ribbon.

Immediately, she lifted her head and looked down the road. Mr. Hendricks was continuing on his way, unaware of what she had just found.

Sarah stepped forward. With trembling knees, she knelt down and picked up the ribbon. It was similar to the ones tied around the scarf and the notes. *But why would Mr. Hendricks have it?*

Sarah tucked the ribbon inside her gray woolen muff and took off down the road after Mr. Hendricks. As she came closer, she wondered what she would say when she caught up with him. For all she knew, the ribbon might have been there all along and might not even belong to Mr. Hendricks. She slowed to a walk, keeping a safe distance behind him.

Sarah's feet ached as she followed him through the streets. She was glad she had worn her clogs to protect her shoes from the soggy ground.

Mr. Hendricks turned left on Marlborough. He passed by Water Street, where he lived, and turned right onto School Street. *Where is he going?* Sarah wondered. Her heart began beating faster as she followed him up the hill toward the Common.

When they had almost reached Tremont Street, Mr. Hendricks slowed down and glanced quickly over his shoulder. Sarah looked down and continued walking. When she looked up, she saw that he had turned left and was heading up the steep, stony path to the stately manor at the top of the hill.

Sarah knew exactly where they were. The two-story mansion was owned by Mr. Richard Clarke, an outspoken Tory and Boston's largest importer of British tea. He sold it at his shop, Richard Clarke & Sons, located at the foot of King Street. *What could Mr. Hendricks want with Mr. Clarke?* she wondered.

Sarah ducked behind one of the towering elms in Mr. Clarke's side yard. She watched, wide-eyed, as Mr. Hendricks marched up the steps to the portico.

The silk damask curtains in the front windows moved aside and Sarah saw a face appear. Before Mr. Hendricks reached the top step, the front door swung open. Mr. Clarke smiled at his visitor as if he had been expecting him.

"Are they still planning to destroy the tea tomorrow night?" Sarah heard Mr. Clarke ask.

Mr. Hendricks nodded. "I just confirmed it with Samuel Adams."

"Well done," said Mr. Clarke. He lifted his chin and turned his head from side to side as if he were looking for something outside. Sarah ducked back behind the tree.

"Do you think you were followed?"

"No," replied Mr. Hendricks. "No one suspects anything."

"Very well then. Please come inside."

Sarah stiffened, unable to move. Her mind raced as the pieces to the puzzle began to fall into place. Mr. Hendricks—the close friend of her father and of Mr. Adams—was working undercover as a British sympathizer. A traitor! Sarah felt sick to her stomach.

She recalled the day of the quilting party when she saw Mr. Hendricks coming out of the Adams's house just moments before she arrived. He had had plenty of time to plant that note. And the other notes—the one on the woodpile and the one wedged into the door—could have easily been placed there by Mr. Hendricks; he was always in and around the coffee house.

She realized that Mr. Hendricks must have been there the night of the massacre, watching as the British soldiers gunned down Patrick and the others. Mr. Clarke must have paid for his silence at the trial. *So the scarf and the notes—to Mr. Hendricks, they were merely opportunities to earn money at the expense of me and my family! What a desperate, greedy soul to sell himself so easily!*

Sarah heard Mr. Clarke's front door close. *I need help,* she told herself. *Mr. Clarke knows all about tomorrow night. If I don't stop him, Papa and the other men involved could be killed!*

Sarah stared at the windows in Mr. Clarke's house. There was no movement. She took a deep breath and dashed out from behind the tree. She didn't stop running until she reached Purchase Street.

She darted up the path and rapped on the Adams's door. It seemed to take forever before the door finally opened.

"Hello, Miss Turner," said Sam Jr. His smile vanished when he saw the desperate expression on Sarah's face.

"I had hoped to speak to your father," she said, panting. "It's important. I—" She stopped, not knowing where to begin. Sam ushered her inside. "What is it?"

Sarah took a deep breath and began to tell Sam

everything, beginning with the night of the massacre. This time, however, she didn't care what anyone thought about her breaking curfew. All she cared about was protecting the lives of the men who would be involved tomorrow night.

Sam nodded in agreement. "There's no time to waste." He stood up and glanced out the window. "Soon it will be dark. There's no time to find my father, or yours. We must stop Mr. Clarke now before it's too late."

"But how?" asked Sarah.

"Come with me," he said, pulling on his cloak. "I have an idea. We'll pay Mr. Hendricks a visit."

8

THE CONFRONTATION

LONG SHADOWS STRETCHED ALONG THE ground as the sun dipped down in the gray December sky. Sarah stood next to Sam in front of Mr. Hendricks's house as they waited for his return.

"There he is," said Sam in a low voice. Sarah saw the faint outline of a figure coming up the road. "Quick, hide behind that tree until I tell you to come out. This could be dangerous."

Sarah crouched down behind the tree. She wrapped her arms around her knees and prayed in silence.

"Well, what brings you here, Master Adams?" called Mr. Hendricks as he stepped onto his front yard.

Sarah peeked out from behind the tree. Sam wasn't smiling. "I'm afraid I have some rather serious business to discuss with you, sir."

"Well, then, why don't you come in and have a

seat? I'm sure—"

"No," Sam interrupted curtly. "That won't be necessary."

There was a long pause. Sarah shut her eyes and continued to pray.

"I have information that you are not who you say you are, Mr. Hendricks."

"Why, whatever do you mean?"

"You may play the role of a devoted Whig, but you're no Whig. Isn't that right, *sir*?"

Sarah peered out. Mr. Hendricks stepped closer to Sam. "Those are pretty strong words, son. I don't think your father would be pleased if he found his son talking this way to one of his comrades, do you?"

Sam stood his ground, folding his arms across his chest. "I asked you a question, sir."

Mr. Hendricks looked over his shoulder and then back at Sam. He took another step closer and pointed his finger at Sam's face. "Perhaps you didn't hear me, boy. You best keep your nose out of places that don't concern you."

Sarah swallowed. She looked up and down Water Street for any sign of help in case things got out of hand. She spotted a small stagecoach pulled by two horses, but it was headed in the wrong direction. Fear knotted her stomach and made her head throb. She realized they were all alone.

Mr. Hendricks glared at Sam. "Get off my property before I—"

Sarah could hold out no longer. Despite Sam's instruction to the contrary, she stepped out from behind the tree. In a voice not quite so steady, she blurted out, "I know, Mr. Hendricks, that you left the scarf and the threatening notes. I saw you enter Mr. Clarke's house. I know you're selling secrets to the Tories."

Mr. Hendricks stood silent with his mouth open, staring in disbelief.

"We have demands," added Sam, "and if you don't comply, we'll expose you to the colonists for what you really are: a traitor!"

There was a long pause. Mr. Hendricks studied Sarah and then Sam. The muscles in his face were tight. "What do you want from me?" he asked darkly.

"Tell Clarke to keep the details about tomorrow's event a secret from the rest of the Tories," said Sam. "If they find out, it could—"

"I'm afraid it's too late for that," said Mr. Hendricks, sneering. "Mr. Clarke already has a plan in place to foil your father's scheme tomorrow night."

"Then go back and tell him something—anything—to divert him," said Sam. "Tell Mr. Clarke that you just met with my father and he informed you that he has changed his mind. Tell him that he's just learned that information has been leaked and he has no choice now but to cancel everything."

Mr. Hendricks shook his head. "What makes you think he'll believe me?"

"He's believed you all along, hasn't he?"

No one spoke a word for several seconds. Sam, still standing with his arms folded, stared at Mr. Hendricks and waited for his response. Sarah stood next to Sam and tried her best to look older than she was.

Mr. Hendricks's eyes shifted nervously to Sam, then to Sarah, then back to Sam. Sarah knew he was trying to decide whether they had enough proof and enough resolve to expose him as a traitor. To Sarah, the answer seemed obvious. Sam was the son of the most influential Whig in all of Boston. And Mr. Hendricks would be foolish to think the offense would go unpunished. After all, if the Whigs were not afraid to stand up to England and destroy one of her most valuable commodities, tea, then they wouldn't hesitate to come after a traitor within their own ranks.

Mr. Hendricks pursed his lips tightly. "All right," he said at last. "I'll do it."

A rush of relief left Sarah dizzy.

"Very well," said Sam. Staring intently into Mr. Hendricks's steel gray eyes, he said, "Remember, you won't survive a day in this town if you're uncovered."

Sam nodded to Sarah, and together they headed toward King Street. Neither of them dared look back. "We need to find our fathers and tell them what just happened," said Sam.

"But—"

"Don't worry, Sarah," said Sam, placing his hand on her shoulder. "I won't tell them about the night of the massacre. That will be our secret."

Sarah smiled, grateful that Sam understood—and that she could trust him.

They walked along until Sarah finally broke the silence. "Sam," she said in a firm voice, "I must be a part of the mission tomorrow night."

Sam looked at Sarah, then turned away and continued to walk in silence.

"Now that you know my past," she continued, "you can understand how miserable I've been, knowing that I failed to stand up to the English soldiers after watching them take Patrick's life. Now's my chance to do something right—and this time I won't fail."

Sam stopped and turned to her. "Sarah, you were only eight years old, just a child! You can't spend the rest of your life blaming yourself. Besides, there are too many risks involved, especially now that the Tories know of our plan. And don't be too quick to believe what Mr. Hendricks said. He's a born liar. He may not do what he has promised."

Sarah had already considered that possibility, but hearing Sam say it was like a splash of cold water in her face. Still, nothing could change her mind.

Sam's face softened as he studied Sarah's. "Well, I don't think I could stop you even if I tried." He smiled. "Patrick was right. You aren't like other girls."

Sarah felt her cheeks flush. "Then you'll help me?"

"I suppose I have to. Just promise that you'll be careful."

9

THE SHIPS REMAIN

IT WAS MONDAY MORNING, DECEMBER 16TH. The deadline for the ships to leave Boston had arrived.

Sarah jumped out of bed and looked out the window toward the harbor. The ships hadn't moved, for she could still see the tips of their masts just over the treetops.

As Sarah swept the floor and began preparing fresh cornbread to serve in the coffee house, she rehearsed the details of her own secret plan repeatedly in her mind. She had carefully planned her disguise as a Mohawk Indian, including how she would hide her long, auburn hair.

Minutes seemed like hours as Sarah grew restless with anticipation.

As darkness fell, she had no appetite for supper. After all, this was the most important night of her life. Fighting for her fallen cousin, for her rights as a colonist, and to save the family business from possible ruin was worth any risk, however great.

Many thoughts ran through her mind as she considered the dangers involved. *Did Mr. Hendricks tell Mr. Clarke that the plan is off? And even if he did, will Mr. Clarke believe him?* She thought about her mother and how worried she would be if she found her only child missing that night. *I'll leave a candle burning in my chamber,* she decided. *She'll see the light under my door and think I'm reading or getting ready for bed.*

"Boston Harbor a teapot tonight!" shouted someone outside. *This is no tea party,* thought Sarah, as she imagined all that could go wrong.

The ominous peal of church bells echoed outside her window. She counted the chimes. It was time.

Sarah tiptoed from her bedchamber to the coffee house. The only glimmer of light in the shop came from the flickering lanterns on King Street. Feeling her way toward the back of the shop, Sarah stepped out the back door and looked for the burlap sack Sam said he'd leave for her. She picked it up and carried it inside.

She opened the sack and dumped the contents on the table. There were some of Sam's old clothes: a pair of knee-length breeches and a white ruffled shirt. In order for her disguise to work, Sarah knew that she would need to dress like a boy before she dressed like an Indian.

There, alone in the cold, dark coffee house, Sarah began to get dressed. It took forever to unbutton her dress and remove the layers of undergarments. *Men have it so easy,* she told herself as she held the breeches up to her hoop frame.

The breeches hung loosely on her hips and the sleeves on the shirt were too long. She rolled the sleeves up high on her elbow. As part of her disguise, Sarah left her legs and feet bare. Tiny goosebumps quickly covered her pale, thin legs. Her body began to shiver. *Was it the cold or her nerves? Probably both,* she decided.

To darken her face, Sarah dipped her fingers into a basin of chimney soot she had collected earlier that day. Her hands trembled as she rubbed the ashes over her hair, face, neck, hands, and lower legs.

To cover her clothes, she draped an old blanket over her shoulders and tied it around her waist with a piece of rope. Then she tied a black ribbon around her hair at the base of her neck and tucked the ponytail into her shirt collar.

There was only one thing left to do. In the still darkness, she kneeled and prayed to God for courage and safety.

Soon Sarah heard a faint rustling sound. It seemed to be coming up the street, perhaps near

Boston's Town House. Sarah's heart pounded faster and faster as the sound grew louder and louder.

Slowly she cracked open the shop door and peered out. Coming toward her was an awesome sight! One hundred and fifty men dressed as Mohawk Indians were marching side by side, as if prepared for battle.

There were men of all shapes and sizes. Most had darkened their faces, and some were even wearing face paint and feathers. A few men carried axes, but no one was armed with a gun.

So many men, Sarah observed. *No one will try to stop us!* As the "Indians" approached the coffee house, Sarah took a deep breath and got into position.

This is it.

10

THE BOSTON TEA PARTY

HER TIMING WOULD HAVE TO BE PERFECT. Her execution, flawless. There was no room for mistakes.

Just as the group passed the coffee house, Sarah slipped into the middle of the pack, marching in step with the others. *Good. No one seemed to notice her.*

She was breathing a sigh of relief when someone jabbed her in the shoulder. "Hey, you!" shouted one of the men behind her. Sarah froze. Some of the men turned to stare at her as they marched by.

Trembling, Sarah looked up and saw a large man with a blackened face glaring at her. She did not speak.

"What do you think you're doing here, boy? Do you think this is a game?"

Sarah shook her head furiously.

"You don't belong here," he sneered. "And

whose boy are you, anyway?"

"Let him go," said a familiar voice, marching up from behind. It was Sam. He clapped a hand on Sarah's shoulder. "The more men we have, the better."

The two men exchanged looks. Then the man pointed his finger at Sarah's face. "I'll be watchin' you, boy. One stupid move and I'll turn you loose to the redcoats, understand?"

Sarah felt nauseous. The muscles in her shoulders tightened as she marched onward. She winced with pain as tiny pebbles pierced the bottoms of her bare feet. Her frozen toes felt like blocks of wood.

As she marched on, she wondered if her mother was sleeping or, worse, if she had gone into Sarah's chamber, perhaps to wish her good night. *Knowing what danger Papa and the other Whigs may be facing tonight, I doubt she's sleeping,* Sarah told herself.

The streets were mostly empty except for a few townspeople who had undoubtedly heard the commotion and had come out to investigate. Sarah continued to face forward, hoping to blend in with everyone else.

The sight of the harbor up ahead sent a chill down Sarah's spine. The moon shone mysteriously on the red waistcoats of the soldiers standing guard in front of the ships. All at once Sarah was transported back to the night of the massacre.

Tonight, like that night, the air was raw and still. She pictured how Patrick must have looked that night, lying in the snow with blood trickling from his wound. But tonight, along with fear, Sarah felt great strength and determination. Nothing could stop her as she marched confidently toward the ships.

When they had almost reached the harbor, Sarah's eyes caught sight of Mr. Hendricks standing behind a small crowd of people who had gathered along the waterfront. He was alone. He appeared nervous as he scanned the troop of Indians marching past. *But where is Mr. Clarke? Is he hiding with the rest of the Tories, waiting for a signal from Mr. Hendricks to make their attack?* Sarah's eyes searched the alleys between the buildings as she continued on her way.

When they reached Griffin's Wharf, one of the men divided the Indians into three groups. Each group was assigned to one of the three ships. Sarah's group was assigned to the *Dartmouth.*

She followed orders and boarded the ship in an orderly fashion. She marched right past a soldier standing guard. He looked stunned and did not offer any resistance.

Sarah listened to the haunting sound of feet shuffling on the ship's deck. She remembered Mr. Adams's instruction to make this a peaceful, orderly mission. *So far, so good.*

Sarah was stationed on the starboard gangway and told to keep watch. Water lapped softly against the ship as she scanned the wharf for any sign of trouble. Then her heart began pounding faster as she peered into the crowd. *Where was Mr. Hendricks?* He had vanished.

As the British crewmen and a handful of soldiers stood by, Sam and the rest of the Indians hoisted the cases of tea onto the deck. A tall, muscular man with a dark beard swung his axe, plunging the sharp blade into the first wooden tea chest. Sarah heard the sound of wood cracking as the other chests were opened. A gentle breeze blew over the ship, and Sarah smelled the delicate aroma of dried tea leaves.

Within minutes the first chest was tipped on its side, allowing the tea to spill into the harbor. Sarah clasped her hands together and, with a grateful heart, looked up toward heaven. There were no cheers, no words from the men on board, only quiet, determined smiles.

More men armed with axes chopped away at the huge tea chests. Sarah watched as her comrades did the same thing on the other two ships.

When the last tea chest was emptied into the harbor, Sarah heard the ghostly chimes of church bells striking twelve times.

She felt a tap on her shoulder. She turned around. One of her fellow Indians shoved a broom in her hand. She looked at the man's darkened face.

It was her father!

She grabbed the broom and, with her head down, immediately began sweeping up the broken crates as commanded. Her cheeks flushed beneath the black soot. *Did he recognize her?* Her stomach churned with the slightest motion of the vessel. As she swept, her father directed the cleanup with the rest of the crew. Nothing suggested he had recognized his daughter. Sarah breathed a sigh of relief and continued her work.

After the crew finished sweeping up the spilled tea and wood fragments, Sarah's group was led off the ship. As they marched down the ramp, the spectators suddenly burst into loud cheers, unable to hold back their enthusiasm any longer. Sarah searched the crowd again, but there was still no sign of Mr. Hendricks or Mr. Clarke.

Once her feet hit dry ground, Sarah disappeared into the darkness, running straight up King Street as fast as she could.

She dodged people as they celebrated and cheered. Indeed, there was much to be thankful for. The tea had been destroyed, and no one had been hurt.

Mission accomplished!

No one in Boston was more relieved than Sarah. For tonight held a much deeper meaning for her. Participating in what would later become known as the *Boston Tea Party* was a personal triumph. Still, Sarah knew something wasn't right. She had known as soon as she had looked into her father's eyes on the deck of the *Dartmouth.* There was one more thing she needed to do.

When she finally reached home, Sarah scrubbed the soot from her face and hands. Then, taking a seat at one of the tables in the coffee house, she waited for her father's return.

"Sarah?" It was her mother, standing in the doorway to the kitchen. Mrs. Turner took one look at Sarah's odd clothing and gasped.

"Yes, it's me, Mama," Sarah answered in a low voice.

"What on God's green earth are you—"

Just then, Sarah's father walked through the front door. His face was black as coal. Drops of perspiration dotted his forehead and arms.

Seth Turner stared at his daughter, saying nothing. Sarah's throat was so dry she could hardly swallow.

"Papa, I'm so sorry." She glanced up at her mother. "Please, sit down, both of you. There is much I need to tell you."

Seth and Isabel looked at each other and then joined their daughter at the table. They listened as Sarah recounted the whole story, beginning with the night of the massacre. Her mother wept softly when Sarah described the sound of the soldiers' guns as they fired into the crowd, killing Patrick. Her father sat solemnly, without emotion, as Sarah described the anonymous notes and the threats to the family business.

Finally, she told them about Mr. Hendricks and how he had been spying for the Tories. Her mother shook her head in disbelief. Her father only bowed his head in silence.

She had almost finished her story when there was a loud knock on the door. Mr. Turner got up from the table to open it. It was Sam Jr.

"Good evening, Mr. Turner. I'm sorry to bother you at this late hour, but I was looking for—oh, there you are, Miss Turner! I've been looking all over for you."

"I'm sorry," said Sarah. "I came right home. What about Mr. Hendricks? Is he still out there?"

"Don't worry about him," said Sam, smiling. "He kept his promise to us and told Mr. Clarke the mission was off. Now he knows Mr. Clarke will be looking for him. I'm sure we've seen the last of him."

Sarah's father looked at Sam. "Thank you for

protecting my daughter tonight and for confronting Mr. Hendricks. You're a brave young man, Master Adams."

Sarah looked at Sam and smiled. Suddenly she was aware that her parents were watching her. She blushed.

Her father smiled and turned back toward Sam. "Would you be our guest for supper tomorrow night?"

"What a fine idea," said her mother excitedly. "We'll have roasted salmon, sweet potatoes, and plum pudding—Sarah's favorite."

Sam smiled graciously. "I'd be honored to join you, Madam Turner."

"Very well," said her father. "And Sarah," he said, turning toward his daughter, "thanks to your courage, many lives were saved tonight. I'm proud of you."

"As am I," said her mother. "It takes a mature young lady to stand up for her family and her beliefs. And I know how difficult it must have been to suffer for three years with that terrible secret and—"

But her mother's voice had begun to fade in Sarah's head. Instead, Sarah's thoughts were focused on one person: Patrick.

Of course, Patrick had consumed most of her thoughts lately. This time, however, his image was different. This time he looked down at her from heaven. He was strong and healthy, just the way she remembered him. And he was pleased, knowing Sarah had done right.